Little Black Sambo

BY HELEN BANNERMAN

Illustrated by EULALIE

Platt & Munk, Publishers/New York

A Division of Grosset & Dunlap

1983 PRINTING
Copyright © 1925,1928, 1955, and 1972
by Platt & Munk, Publishers.
All rights reserved.
Printed in the United States of America.
Published simultaneously in Canada.

Library of Congress Catalog Card Number 79-63963

ISBN: 0-448-49608-9 (Paperback)
ISBN: 0-448-40354-4 (Hardbound)
ISBN: 0-448-13137-4 (Library)

Once upon a time a little boy lived in India, and his name was Little Black Sambo. And his mother was called Mama Sari. And his father was called Papa Simbu.

And Mama Sari made him a beautiful red coat and a pair of beautiful blue trousers.

And Papa Simbu went to the bazaar and bought him a beautiful green umbrella and a lovely little pair of purple shoes with crimson soles and crimson linings.

Little Black Sambo put on all his fine clothes and went out for a walk in the jungle. And by and by he met a tiger. And the tiger said to him, "Little Black Sambo, I'm going to eat you up!"

And Little Black Sambo said, "Oh! Please, Mr. Tiger, don't eat me up. I'll give you my beautiful little red coat."

So the tiger said, "Very well, I won't eat you this time." And it took poor Little Black Sambo's beautiful little red coat, and it went away, saying, "Now I'm the grandest tiger in the jungle."

And Little Black Sambo went on, and by and by he met another tiger, and it said to him, "Little Black Sambo, I'm going to eat you up!"

And Little Black Sambo said, "Oh! Please, Mr. Tiger, don't eat me up. I'll give you my beautiful blue trousers."

So the tiger said, "Very well, I won't eat you this time." And it took poor Little Black Sambo's beautiful blue trousers and went away, saying, "Now I'm the grandest tiger in the jungle."

And Little Black Sambo went on, and by and by he met another tiger, and it said to him, "Little Black Sambo, I'm going to eat you up!"

And Little Black Sambo said, "Oh! Please, Mr. Tiger, don't eat me up. I'll give you my beautiful little purple shoes with crimson soles and crimson linings."

But the tiger said, "What use would your shoes be to me? I have four feet, and you've only two. You haven't enough shoes for me."

And Little Black Sambo said, "You could wear them on your ears."

"So I could," said the tiger. "Give them to me, and I won't eat you this time." So he took poor Little Black Sambo's beautiful little purple shoes with crimson soles and crimson linings and went away, saying, "Now I'm the grandest tiger in the jungle."

And by and by Little Black Sambo met another tiger, and it said to him, "Little Black Sambo, I'm going to eat you up!"

And Little Black Sambo said, "Oh! Please, Mr. Tiger, don't eat me up. I'll give you my beautiful green umbrella."

But the tiger said, "How can I carry an umbrella, when I need all my paws for walking?"

"You could tie it on your tail and carry it that way," said
Little Black Sambo.

"So I could," said the tiger. "Give it to me, and I won't
eat you this time." So he took poor Little Black Sambo's
beautiful green umbrella and went away, saying, "Now I'm
the grandest tiger in the jungle."

And poor Little Black Sambo went away crying, because the tigers had taken all his fine clothes.

Presently he heard a horrible noise that sounded like
"G-r-r-rrrrrr," and it grew louder and louder. "Oh, dear!"
said Little Black Sambo. "All the tigers are coming back to
eat me up!" So he ran to a palm tree and peeped around—

and there he saw all the tigers arguing over which of them was the grandest. They all became so angry that they jumped up and took off the fine clothes and began to tear each other with their claws and bite each other with their big white teeth.

And they came rolling and tumbling to the foot of the very tree where Little Black Sambo was hiding, but he jumped quickly away behind another tree. And the tigers all caught hold of each other's tails, and they wrangled and scrambled.

And soon they found themselves in a ring around the tree.

Then Little Black Sambo jumped up and called out, "Oh, tigers! Why have you taken off all your nice clothes? Don't you want them?"

But the tigers only answered, "G-r-r-rrrr!"

Then Little Black Sambo said, "If you want them, say so, or I'll take them back."

But the tigers would not let go of each other's tails, and so they could only say, "G-r-r-rrrr!"

So Little Black Sambo put on all his fine clothes again.
And the tigers became very, very angry, but still they
would not let go of each other's tails. And they became so
angry that they ran around the tree, trying to eat each other
up.

And they ran faster and faster, till they were whirling so fast Little Black Sambo couldn't see their legs at all.

And still they ran faster and faster, till they all just melted away, and there was nothing left but a great big pool of melted butter round the foot of the tree.

Now, Papa Simbu was just coming home from work with a great big brass pot in his arms, and when he saw what was left of all the tigers he said, "Oh! What lovely melted butter!"

So he put it all into the great big brass pot and took it home to Mama Sari.

When Mama Sari saw the melted butter, wasn't she pleased! "Now," she said, "we'll all have pancakes for supper!"

So Mama Sari made pancake batter. And she fried it in the melted butter which the tigers had made, and out came pancakes just as yellow and brown as little tigers.

And then they all sat down to supper. And Mama Sari ate twenty-seven pancakes, and Papa Simbu ate fifty-five, but Little Black Sambo ate one hundred and sixty-three, because he was so hungry!